MY FIRST
Raggedy

Ann

*Raggedy Ann and Andy
and the Nice Police Officer*

ADAPTED FROM THE STORY BY
JOHNNY GRUELLE

ILLUSTRATED BY JAN PALMER

ALADDIN PAPERBACKS
NEW YORK   LONDON   TORONTO   SYDNEY   SINGAPORE

Weekly Reader is a registered trademark of the Weekly Reader Corporation.

2003 Edition

First Aladdin Paperbacks edition November 2002

Copyright © 1942 by The Johnny Gruelle Company
Adaptation copyright © 1999 by Simon & Schuster, Inc.
Illustrations copyright © 1999 by Simon & Schuster, Inc.
Based on the story *Raggedy Ann and Andy and the Nice Fat Policeman* by Johnny Gruelle.
The names and depictions of Raggedy Ann and Raggedy Andy are trademarks of Simon & Schuster, Inc.

Aladdin Paperbacks
An imprint of Simon & Schuster
Children's Publishing Division
1230 Avenue of the Americas
New York, NY 10020

Also available in a Simon & Schuster Books for Young Readers hardcover edition.
The text of this book was set in Adobe Jenson.
The illustrations were rendered in Winsor and Newton ink and watercolor.

The Library of Congress has cataloged the hardcover edition as follows:
My first Raggedy Ann : Raggedy Ann's and Andy and the nice police officer / adapted from the story by Johnny Gruelle ;
illustrated by Jan Palmer. —1st ed.
          p. cm.
Summary: Raggedy Ann and her brother keep an innocent man from being arrested and help reform a greedy magician..
ISBN 0-689-82174-3 (hc.)
[1. Dolls—Fiction. 2. Police—fiction. 3. Magic—Fiction.] I. Gruelle, Johnny, 1880?-1938.
Raggedy Ann and Andy and the nice fat policeman. II. Palmer, Jan, ill.
PZ7.M9763 1999
[E]—dc21
98-36200
CIP
AC
ISBN 0-689-85344-0 (Aladdin pbk.)

Printed in the United States

The History of Raggedy Ann

One day, a little girl named Marcella discovered an old rag doll in her attic. Because Marcella was often ill and had to spend much of her time at home, her father, a writer named Johnny Gruelle, looked for ways to keep her entertained. He was inspired by Marcella's rag doll, which had bright shoe-button eyes and red yarn hair. The doll became known as Raggedy Ann.

Knowing how much Marcella adored Raggedy Ann, Johnny Gruelle wrote stories about the doll. He later collected the stories he had written for Marcella and published them in a series of books. He gave Raggedy Ann a brother, Raggedy Andy, and over the years the two rag dolls acquired many friends.

Raggedy Ann has been an important part of Americana for more than half a century, as well as a treasured friend to many generations of readers. After all, she is much more than a rag doll—she is a symbol of caring and love, of compassion and generosity. Her magical world is one that promises to delight children of all ages for years to come.

It was a lovely day in June. The birds were singing, the bees were buzzing, and the air was filled with the perfume of flowers. Raggedy Andy took Raggedy Ann's hand and they set off into the deep, deep woods in search of adventure. They found a cool, green path that they had never seen before, and they soon arrived in a clearing.

"Boo-hoo, Boo-hoo."

"Listen," said Raggedy Andy. "Someone is crying." He pointed to a pretty little house with a red roof and flowers growing in the yard. A nice-looking policeman sat on the front step, sobbing into his hands.

Raggedy Ann said, "Let's see if we can help."

When the policeman saw the two rag dolls, he sobbed
louder than ever.

"Mercy me," Raggedy Ann said. "Why are you crying so,
Mr. Police Officer?"

"Oh, it is too sad," he replied. "I found a note on my front
door that said, 'Please arrest Mr. Hooligooly.' I have never
arrested anyone before!"

"Perhaps someone is angry with Mr. Hooligooly and would like to get him into trouble," Raggedy Ann mused. "Maybe he hasn't done anything wrong."

"That is true," the police officer said. A smile came to his face as Raggedy Ann dried the last of his tears.

"Let's go see Mr. Hooligooly," she suggested.

When they reached the front steps of the Hooligooly house, the policeman caught Raggedy Ann's arm. "I don't want to arrest Mr. Hooligooly today," he pleaded. "Let's go back to my house."

"I'll knock on the door," said Raggedy Andy. He wiggled his shoe-button eyes and knocked once, twice, then a third time.

"Who's there?" called Mr. Hooligooly.

"You see! Now you have done it," the policeman wailed. He would have run home if Raggedy Ann had not held on to his coattails.

"This nice police officer is here to arrest you," explained Raggedy Andy.

"Maybe you'd better come in," Mr. Hooligooly said politely.

Raggedy Ann liked the Hooligoolys the minute she saw them. They had cheery smiles and merry twinkles in their eyes.

After they all had finished a snack of cream puffs and lemonade, Mr. Hooligooly said, "Now, why were you going to arrest me?"

Before the police officer could start crying again, Raggedy Andy explained about the note.

"We know who pinned the note to the door," Mrs. Hooligooly said quickly. "A long time ago, Mr. Hooligooly met a little man who followed him home from the forest, and we think he wants our magic cooking stick. It burns in the fireplace, but it never burns up, and it always cooks our food just right. The little man is a magician, and he wants all the magical things in the deep, deep woods."

"Let's go to the magician's house and tell him he can't behave that way," Raggedy Andy suggested.

Mr. Hooligooly said, "What a good idea." They left the Hooligoolys' house with the nice police officer, who would rather have stayed home and helped Mrs. Hooligooly cook dinner. Raggedy Ann stayed with Mrs. Hooligooly, for she was very curious about the magic cooking stick.

At the magician's house, Raggedy Andy climbed up on the roof and disappeared down the chimney. He planned to unlock the door from the inside. When he didn't reappear, Mr. Hooligooly knocked on the door.

"Run home to your mama," called the magician. "I'm holding your friend prisoner."

"We have come to arrest you," said the nice police officer bravely.

Suddenly the door opened, and two pancakes rolled out and landed in front of Mr. Hooligooly and the policeman.

Now they had no idea that these were magic pancakes. For just a moment, they forgot all about their friend Raggedy Andy.

"It is just dandy to have pancakes roll right into our laps," said the nice police officer.

"It surely is," said Mr. Hooligooly, as he took a bite of his pancake.

As soon as Mr. Hooligooly and the policeman bit into their pancakes, they turned into little squealy pigs and . . .

ran
right
home
to Mrs. Hooligooly.

Raggedy Ann and Mrs. Hooligooly were making lovely doughnuts and cream pies when two little squealy pigs ran into the house. The pigs were dressed in Mr. Hooligooly's and the police officer's clothes.

"Mercy me!" said Mrs. Hooligooly, who was about to shoo the pigs outside with her broom.

"Stop, Mrs. Hooligooly," cried Raggedy Ann. "Look at their clothes!
That's Mr. Hooligooly and the police officer!"

Raggedy Ann quickly closed the door. She saw a piece of a pancake sliding out of one pig's pocket. After breaking the pancake into tiny pieces, Raggedy Ann sprinkled it on top of a whipped-cream pie. She opened the front door and put the delicious-looking pie on the steps. Then she closed the door again.

In just a minute, Raggedy Ann opened the door, and a third little pig ran inside the house, dressed in the magician's clothes. "There!" said Raggedy Ann. "I knew the magician would be lurking outside. I gave him some of his own medicine."

"But how do we change them back?" said Mrs. Hooligooly. "I don't like to have pigs in my parlor, even if one of them is my husband. And I'm sure they don't enjoy being pigs."

"If we go to the magician's house, we can hunt through his magic books and find out how to change them back," Raggedy Ann replied. "Do you want to come with us?" she asked the pigs.

All three pigs squealed so loudly that Mrs. Hooligooly held her hands over her ears. Raggedy Ann locked the magician pig in the cellar. Then she and Mrs. Hooligooly led the other two pigs to the magician's house.

The magician had left Raggedy Andy hanging on a hook by the fireplace. This didn't hurt his soft rag body, but he wished he could help his friends. While Raggedy Ann set him loose, Mrs. Hooligooly found the magician's red book on the kitchen table. She and Raggedy Ann read a magic spell from the book and changed the police officer and Mr. Hooligooly back into themselves.

"My goodness!" said Mr. Hooligooly. "I will never eat another pancake that appears out of nowhere." The friends brought the squealy magician pig to jail. Then Raggedy Ann said the spell that changed him back into a magician.

"You'll stay here until you say you're sorry," Raggedy Andy told the magician. "Our friend, the police officer, will stop by after dinner and look in on you." Then Raggedy Ann and Raggedy Andy, the Hooligoolys, and the nice police officer left the jail and went back to the house, where they cooked a delicious turkey dinner with the magic cooking stick.

After dinner, Raggedy Ann and Raggedy Andy went with the policeman to the jail, where they found the magician looking very sad. "I'm sorry," he said. "I used to be a grocer, until I found the magic book. Then I became very greedy and wanted everything that was magic. Now I just want to have friends again."

Raggedy Ann and Raggedy Andy looked at each other, and their shoe-button eyes twinkled with happiness.

"We are very glad," Raggedy Ann said, "for there is nothing that brings such happiness as friendship. We will let you go home and keep the magic book, as long as you wish for lovely things for others. What better way to make new friends!"

The magician promised he would, and the nice police officer let him out of jail. They all said good night, and the two rag dolls went home to their friends in the nursery.